The Perfect Spot

ROBERT J. BLAKE

PHILOMEL BOOKS
NEW YORK

Copyright © 1992 by Robert J. Blake.
All rights reserved. This book, or parts thereof, may not be
reproduced in any form without permission from the publisher.
Philomel Books, a division of The Putnam & Grosset Book Group,
200 Madison Avenue, New York, NY 10016.   Published simultaneously in Canada.
Printed in Hong Kong by South China Printing Co. (1988) Ltd.
Book design by Nanette Stevenson. Lettering by David Gatti.
The text is set in Sabon.

Library of Congress Cataloging-in-Publication Data
Blake, Robert J.   The perfect spot / by Robert J. Blake.
p.   cm.   Summary: A father and his son take great care searching the woods
for the perfect spot for the father to paint a picture
and the boy to catch insects and frogs.
ISBN 0-399-22132-8
[1. Nature—Fiction. 2. Fathers and sons—Fiction.] I. Title.
PZ7.B564Pe   1992   91-16006 CIP AC   [E]—dc20

First Impression

For my father from his son,
for my son from his father

When Dad goes into the woods, he brings his paints, his easel, and a big canvas. When I go into the woods with him, I bring a net, a jar, and some shortbread. We share the shortbread.

My dad has been all over the woods looking for just the right scene to make just the right painting. He likes oak trees, shadows, rocks, and water.

I have been all over the woods looking for a unicorn beetle, a sphinx caterpillar, and a green cricket frog.

I found a red salamander under a rock.

"Look, Dad," I said. But he was busy. I found an ambush bug and a unicorn beetle, and dropped them into my jar together. "Don't fight, you guys," I told them.

We hurried on. We hadn't found the right spot yet.

"This looks like a good place," I said. There were lots of trees.
"Too gray."
"How about over here?" The shadows were great.
"We did that yesterday."
"Do you like this old stump?"
"I'm not in a stump mood," Dad grumbled.
So we kept walking. A good spot can be hard to find.

We hiked on the trail and off the trail. We climbed up the hill, down through the glen, and over the footbridge. My legs were getting tired.

"Can we stop and look for a frog?"

"Not now!" Dad said.

Then I saw the waterfall.

"How about that?" I asked.

There were trees, rocks, and shadows. Even Dad seemed interested. And on the other side of the water, under a big tree root, was a green cricket frog! I snuck up on it as quietly as I could.

Just as I was about to catch it Dad yelled, "COME ON! LET'S MOVE ON!"

The frog jumped. I jumped. I tried to grab it but I missed. I slipped and fell and I wound up in the stream.

Dad dropped his painting gear, and crossed from rock to rock.
He hit one that I had gotten all wet, slipped, his foot went in, and
he got a soaker.

I sat still and tried to be small. I was sure he was going to yell
at me.

But he didn't. He just started laughing.

He bumped me with his shoulder and I bumped him back. He splashed me and I splashed him back. For a while we ran around and bumped and splashed and laughed.

Then for a while we said nothing.

"Should we move on now?" I asked.
"Why?" he said. "We've found the perfect spot!"

Dad hummed as he set up his easel and began to paint.
I poked around the rocks, and before long, out came the green
cricket frog. We sat and blinked at each other.

I didn't try to catch him this time.